The Dentist
from the
Black Lagoon

by Mike Thaler · pictures by Jared Lee

SCHOLASTIC INC.

New York   Toronto   London   Auckland   Sydney
Mexico City   New Delhi   Hong Kong   Buenos Aires

To Dr. Solberg and Joanne,
only kidding!
—M.T.

To all the friendly dentists everywhere
who take good care of our teeth.
—J.L.

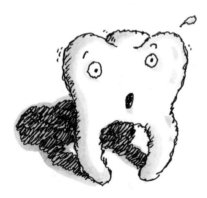

ISBN 0-439-68074-3

Text copyright © 2005 by Mike Thaler.
Illustrations copyright © 2005 by Jared D. Lee Studio, Inc.

12 11 10   7 8 9 10/0

Printed in the U.S.A.
First printing, January 2005

Uh-oh, it's Dental Health month!

SUN

TOOTH FAIRY

Miss Hearse, the nurse, says there's a real dentist coming on Friday. His name is Dr. B.N. Payne.

He's bringing his equipment, and he's going to check our teeth.

I don't want checked teeth . . .

maybe polka-dotted ones.

I'm scared! I heard all dentists have four hands,
two heads, and are *Yank*-ee fans. After your teeth are taken out,
they give you toothpaste to stick 'em back in.

TOOTHPASTE

YANKS

One kid said a dentist gave his cousin gas. I hope it was unleaded.

Then he drilled him.

Another kid said a dentist put *caps* on his brother's teeth.

His mouth must have looked like a Little League team.

Penny said her aunt has *crowns* on hers.

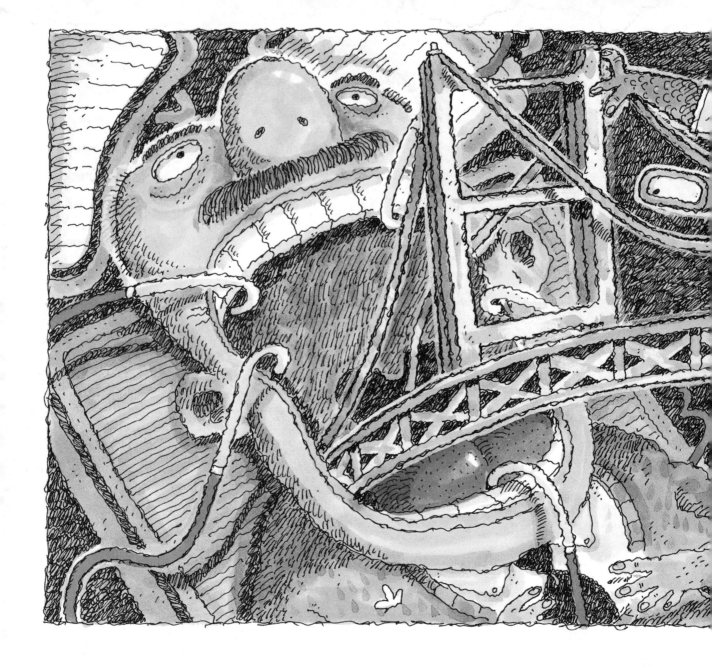

"Big deal," said Derek. "A dentist put a bridge in *my* uncle's mouth."

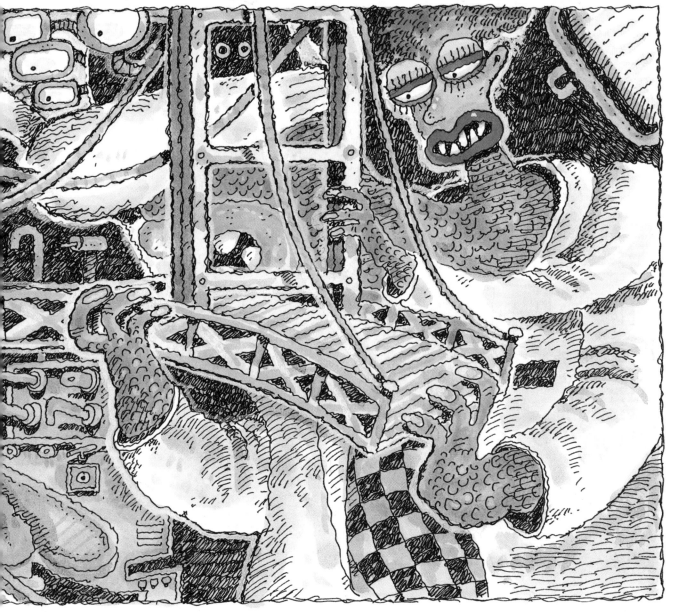

FLOSS

Wow, I hope it wasn't the Golden Gate!

NOODLE

He also said his dad has a whole root canal in his mouth—

sounds *Erie* to me.

My best friend, Eric, is going to a special dinosaur dentist called an *ORTHODON*, who's giving him a good bite.
I told him to brace himself.

My grandpa told me my grandma's teeth are like stars—

they come out at night.

WISDOM TOOTH

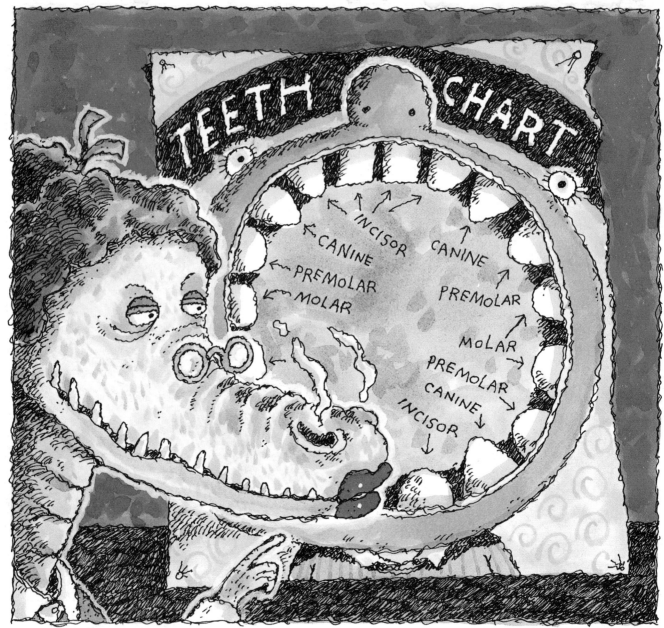

Mrs. Green says each tooth has its own name.

TOOTH ACHE

I thought they all had *my* name and were just called, "Hubie's teeth."

MOLAR POWER

Well, *my* teeth are staying in *my* mouth!

SMILE

Oh, no, we're on our way to the nurse's office.

 We line up by the door and go in—one by one.

I don't hear any screams *yet*. I'm polite and let everyone go ahead of me.
But finally, it's *my* turn. . . .

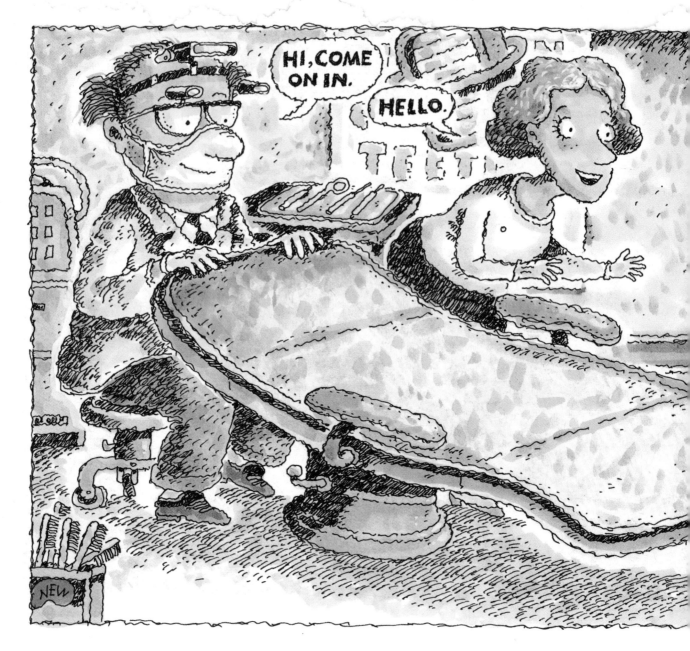

I go in . . . there's a man in a mask sitting there.

And it isn't the Lone Ranger.

LONE
RANGER →

Dr. Payne tells me to open wide and looks in my mouth with a little mirror. Then he pats me on the head, gives me a new toothbrush, and tells me to use it every day.

Hey, that wasn't so bad. I got out of there with all my teeth, a new
toothbrush, and a great big smile!

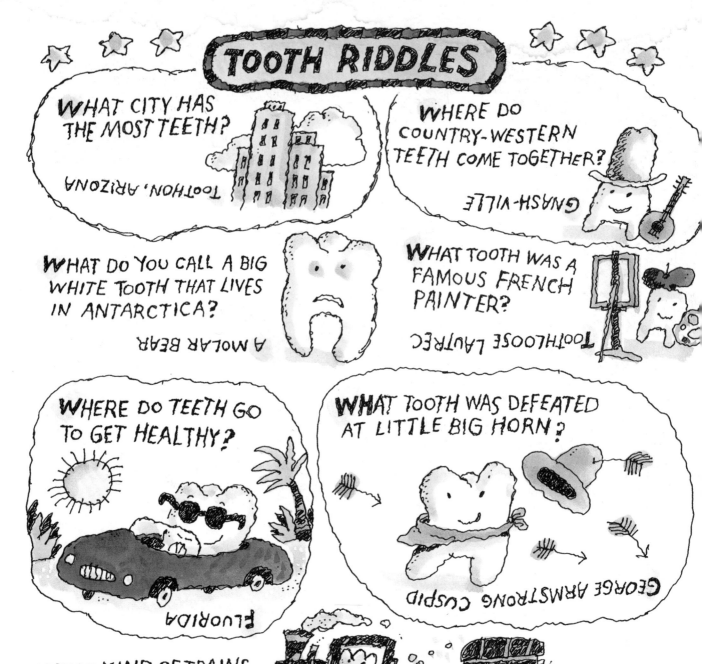